MARVEL
EARTH'S MIGHT
the
AVENGER

**WRITER: Christopher Yost**
**ARTIST: Scott Wegener**
with Patrick Scherberger (Issue #4)

*"TRUST," "MUTUAL RESPECT" & "COURAGE"*
**ARTIST: Patrick Scherberger**
with Sandu Florea (Inker, "Mutual Respect")

COLORIST: Jean-Francois Beaulieu
LETTERERS: Dave Sharpe & VC's Joe Sabino (Issue #3)
COVER ARTISTS: Patrick Scherberger (Issue #3) & Scott Wegener (Issue #4)
EDITORS: Nathan Cosby, Michael Horwitz & Jordan D. White

COLLECTION EDITOR: Cory Levine
EDITORIAL ASSISTANTS: James Emmett & Joe Hochstein
ASSISTANT EDITORS: Matt Masdeu, Alex Starbuck & Nelson Ribeiro
EDITORS, SPECIAL PROJECTS: Jennifer Grünwald & Mark D. Beazley
SENIOR EDITOR, SPECIAL PROJECTS: Jeff Youngquist
SENIOR VICE PRESIDENT OF SALES: David Gabriel
BOOK DESIGN: Patrick McGrath

EDITOR IN CHIEF: Axel Alonso
CHIEF CREATIVE OFFICER: Joe Quesada
PUBLISHER: Dan Buckley
EXECUTIVE PRODUCER: Alan Fine

1

AVENGERS MANSION, NEW YORK CITY.
WHAT YEAR IS IT AGAIN?
PRESENT DAY.

BECAUSE EVERY TIME I COME IN CAPTAIN AMERICA'S ROOM, I GET CONFUSED.
SERIOUSLY, IT'S LIKE A HOTEL ROOM FROM 1940.

1943 ACTUALLY, WASP. GIVE ME SOME CREDIT, I HAD TO CALL PEPPER TWICE TO MAKE HER MAKE THIS HAPPEN.
I'M JUST SAYING, ARE WE SURE THIS IS HEALTHY? I CAN'T EVEN IMAGINE HOW HARD THIS HAS BEEN ON CAP...

...BUT HE'S BEEN UNFROZEN FOR LIKE A MONTH NOW.
HE'S NOT REALLY GETTING OUT THERE AND ADAPTING TO THE PRESENT DAY. OR FUTURE, I GUESS.
IT IS HIS DAY OFF...
WHATEVER. YOU KNOW HE'S OUT THERE, PROBABLY ALL SAD AND MOPING AROUND. HE LOST HIS WHOLE WORLD!!
HE'S PROBABLY HANGING OUT IN A MUSEUM OR SOMETHING.
PARDON ME, SIR... BUT I AM RECEIVING AN INTRUDER ALERT--

REALLY? I'VE GOT A BURGLAR?
INDEED, SIR. EXCEPT THAT THE 'BURGLAR' IN THIS CASE IS THE ADVANCED IDEA MECHANICS.
THEY ARE RAIDING A STARK INDUSTRIES EXPERIMENTAL TECHNOLOGY WAREHOUSE.
WHAT?! JARVIS, YOU COULD HAVE JUST SAID SO.
WASP! WE'VE GOT TO GO!
SIGH.
I WONDER WHAT A SUPER-SOLDIER FROM THE 1940S EVEN DOES ON HIS DAY OFF?

ADAPTATION
TIMES SQUARE, NEW YORK CITY.
DESTROY CAPTAIN AMERICA!

I MUST CONFESS, MON CAPITAN... BATROC ZE LEAPER IS NOT IMPRESSED WITH YOUR MIGHTY SHIELD.
SORRY TO DISAPPOINT, 'BATROC'...
SPTANG

...BUT I WASN'T AIMING FOR YOU.
WHAM!
UHN!!

I DON'T KNOW WHAT YOU AND YOUR CREW ARE PLOTTING...
CREW? I PREFER BRIGADE...
ZARAN!!

...BUT THE AVENGER FILES HAVE YOU FLAGGED AS BAD GUYS. AND WHERE I'M FROM?

TBAM!
WE TAKE BAD GUYS DOWN!

THNK!
WHERE YOU'RE FROM, CAPTAIN? DON'T YOU MEAN 'WHEN' YOU'RE FROM?

AFTER ALL, YOU'RE THE MAN OUT OF TIME...
FIXER, RIGHT? YOU'RE GOING TO HAVE TO DO BETTER THAN A FEW METAL STICKS TO BEAT ME, SON.
OH, DON'T WORRY, CAPTAIN...

...I INTEND TO.
VM!
VM!
FWOOOOSH!!
VM!

UHNN!

ALAS, CAPTAIN...AS MUCH AS MY COUNTRY APPRECIATES YOUR CONTRIBUTION IN THE SECOND GREAT WAR...
...I AM AFRAID THAT ZE CURRENT CIRCUMSTANCES REQUIRE WE BREAK FRANCE'S TREATY WITH YOU.

HN!!
YOU REALLY DIDN'T THINK MY TECH PACK WAS A THREAT, DID YOU? YOU PROBABLY DON'T EVEN KNOW WHAT NANOBOT TECH IS.
FIXER, PLEASE... HE IS VERY OLD, NO? SHOW ZE ELDERLY SOME RESPECT.
AND THEN ELIMINATE HIM.
I MAY NOT BE FAMILIAR WITH YOUR FANCY BLASTERS, MISTER...
GAHH!
UFF!
...BUT I KNOW WHEN SOMEONE IS TALKING TOO MUCH!!

FAP!
POLICE
POLICE

VICTORY IS *YOURS*, CAPTAIN...
...AND YET YOU LOOK AS IF RAGNAROK ITSELF WERE UPON YOU.
*THOR ODINSON* WOULD KNOW WHY.

YOU FOUGHT WELL, FROM THE LOOKS OF THINGS...
NO. I DIDN'T.
I WAS SLOPPY. I GOT DISTRACTED BY THE MAN WITH THE MECHANICAL WEAPONS. HIS TECHNOLOGY... I'VE NEVER SEEN ANYTHING LIKE IT.
I WASN'T READY FOR IT, THOR.
Antonio

Cola
THIS... THIS IS NOT MY WORLD. THIS IS THE *FUTURE.*
I KNOW THAT THERE'S STILL WORK TO DO, THAT IRON MAN SAYS CAPTAIN AMERICA IS STILL NEEDED...
POLICE

...BUT I DON'T KNOW IF I CAN ADAPT TO THIS.
I UNDERSTAND.
IS THAT SO?
AYE. FOR I AM AN IMMORTAL... AND I HAVE WATCHED THIS WORLD CHANGE OVER *THOUSANDS* OF YEARS.

I HAVE WATCHED WHOLE CULTURES BE SWALLOWED UP, WIPED FROM THE EARTH...
...BECAUSE THEY COULD NOT ADAPT.

BUT I DO NOT BELIEVE THAT CAPTAIN AMERICA IS LIKE THEM.
Antonio

...
THOUGH IN TRUTH, I AM NOT A FAN OF MORTAL TECHNOLOGY EITHER. IRON MAN'S 'CARD' ONCE AGAIN BECKONS.
BZZT!
BZZT!
BZZT!

AVENGERS, ASSEMBLE!!

THAT'S STRANGE...MY ID CARD DIDN'T GO OFF.
IRON MAN BELIEVES YOU TO HAVE 'THE DAY OFF,' AS HE CALLS IT. BUT YOU ARE A WARRIOR! AND A WARRIOR DOES NOT VACATION!
FOLLOW ME, CAPTAIN...

...FOR BATTLE IS NEARBY!!

STARK INDUSTRIES WAREHOUSE 410.
THAT'S THE LAST ONE! WE ONLY HAVE 1.2 MINUTES LEFT!
I THINK NOT, VILLAIN!!
OHHHHH, DARN.

IF YOU KNOW WHAT'S GOOD FOR YOU, GENTLEMEN...
...SURRENDER.

YOU THINK WE'RE NOT PREPARED FOR THE AVENGERS? A.I.M. IS COMPOSED OF THE GREATEST MINDS EVER TO WALK THE PLANET! OUR SCIENCE WILL DESTROY YOU!
SEND IT IN!!
THIS IS 221, WE HAVE A SITUATION. SEND IN THE ADAPTOID.

ADAPTOID? YOU MORTALS ARE JUST MAKING UP WORDS NOW, IT WOULD SE--

CHOOOOM!

THOR, ARE YOU ALL RIGHT?
NAY, CAPTAIN, I AM NOT. BUT I WILL BE ONCE I SMITE THESE SCIENTISTS.
WE MAY HAVE A BIGGER PROBLEM...

THIS... THING... IS NO THREAT. I WILL DEAL WITH--
THOR, WAIT. LOOK.

MOVE!!

CAP! WE'VE GOT THIS! WASP, ANT-MAN, HAWKEYE... TAKE THIS GUY OUT!
IRON MAN...

IRON MAN...
IRON MAN, PULL BACK! GET THE AVENGERS OUT OF HERE!

ALL RIGHT, WHATEVER YOU ARE... YOU'VE GOT NO CHANCE HERE. STAND DOWN, AND WE'LL...
IRON MAN, WAIT... PERHAPS WE SHOULD LISTEN TO THE CAPTAIN...
SOMETHING'S HAPPENING...

OKAY, THAT LOOKS BAD. ANYONE HAVE A PLAN?
YEAH.

DUCK!!!

SHOOOM!
NYEARGH!!
AAAHH!

ZZAKOOM!
ARMOR'S ANALYZING... IT'S SOME KIND OF NANO TECH ANDROID--
WASP, WATCH OUT!
WAAH!

HNN!
THOR! TH--

THOOOM!

ONLY WE REMAIN, CAPTAIN... IF WE MEET OUR END THIS DAY, SO BE IT...
...BUT I SWEAR, THIS MACHINE WILL FALL WITH US!!
IT'S A MACHINE... BUT NO MATTER HOW HIGH TECH IT MAY SEEM...
...EVERY MACHINE NEEDS AN ENGINE.
I NEED AN OPENING, THOR...
THEN BY ODIN, YOU SHALL HAVE IT!
HAVE AT THEE, ADAPTOID!!

CRAKAKKK

THUD!!

OKAY, THAT WAS HORRIBLE. WHAT HAPPENED?
SOME KIND OF NANO-GENERATOR, IT WAS ANALYZING AND REPLICATING OUR POWERS MECHANICALLY...
I'M IMPRESSED... THAT'S SOME OF THE MOST ADVANCED TECH I'VE EVER SEEN. APART FROM MINE.
HOW'D YOU KNOW WHERE TO HIT IT, CAP?

NO MATTER HOW MUCH THE WORLD CHANGES, A TRUE WARRIOR FINDS A WAY TO CHANGE WITH IT.
WOULDN'T YOU AGREE, CAPTAIN?

From Wasp!
BEGIN PLAYLIST... GREATEST HITS OF THE 1940S...
CHANGE PLAYLIST... MODERN.
THE END

TRUST ME.
TRUST

IN POINT OF FACT, HAWKEYE... I DO NOT.
ARE YOU SERIOUS, PANTHER?!
SHUT UP! BOTH OF YOU, JUST SHUT UP!
YOU AVENGERS HAVE BEEN CHASING ME EVER SINCE I ESCAPED THE VAULT... BUT I'M NOT GOING BACK!
YOU DON'T TRUST ME?!
HEY! I AM IN CONTROL HERE!! ME!
NO. BUT PLEASE... SHOOT.
FT!!
YOU GOT IT.
NO!

YOU TWO ARE NOTHING! I'VE FOUGHT IRON MAN!!
FT!!
FT!!
FT!!
YEAH, AND HE LOCKED YOU UP IN THE VAULT WHEN YOU WERE DONE. NOW QUIT INTERRUPTING, THE GROWN-UPS ARE SPEAKING!
CHAK!
THERE CAN NEVER BE TRUST WITH A MAN WHO TRUSTS NO ONE.
WHAT IS THAT, ANCIENT 'PANTHER TRIBE' WISDOM?
IT IS.
WELL...WELL, IT GOES BOTH WAYS!!
RAAA!!
ENOUGH WITH THE FIGHTING, YOU IDIOTS! I WANT ANT-MAN AND WASP TO FIGHT ME INSTEAD!!
SHRACK!!

KSHH!
KSSSH!
KSSSH!
KSSHH!
KSSSH!

...WELL, THAT'S JUST GREAT. THIS IS ALL YOUR FAULT, PANTHER.

DO YOU NOT HAVE FLARE ARROWS?
I USED THE LAST ONE SIGNALING YOU TO THIS PLACE.
MAN, I KNEW I SHOULD HAVE DONE THIS SOLO!! WHIPLASH COULD BE RIGHT IN FRONT OF ME AND I WOULDN'T KNOW IT.
HAWKEYE... TRUST ME.

TRUST YOU? THAT'S RICH. TRUST THE GUY THAT BROKE INTO AVENGERS MANSION AND SPIED ON THE TEAM?
WE'RE BOTH GOING TO DIE HERE AND YOU'RE PLAYING GAMES!
I WILL IGNORE THE FACT THAT YOU WERE A SPY FOR S.H.I.E.L.D., BECAUSE EVEN MORE DANGEROUS ARE YOUR EMOTIONS.
YOU ARE RULED BY THEM! YOU ARE RECKLESS, AND LET YOUR EGO MAKE DECISIONS FOR YOU.

BUT PERHAPS WE SHOULD BOTH LEARN TO TRUST, IF WE ARE GOING TO BE ON A TEAM TOGETHER.

WELL, WE MIGHT AS WELL PACK IT IN, YOUR HIGHNESS...
...BECAUSE I'M NOT GOING TO PUT MY LIFE IN YOUR HANDS OR ANY OF THE OTHER AVENGERS!
BEHIND YOU!!
CHAKKK!
RRRRAAAAAAA!

SO...
...YOU TRUSTED ME AFTER ALL.
YEAH... BUT I DIDN'T LIKE IT.
HOW DID YOU KNOW WHERE SHE WAS?
BECAUSE I CAN SEE IN THE DARK.
I'M SORRY, WHAT? DID YOU SAY YOU COULD SEE IN THE DARK?!
I DID.
...
YOU COULD HAVE TOLD ME!!
I TRUSTED THAT YOU KNEW.
END.

THE SKIES OVER SWITZERLAND.
HE'S A RUSSIAN NATIONAL NAMED IVAN VANKO. HE'S A BRILLIANT ENGINEER THAT CREATED A SUIT OF ARMOR SIMILAR TO IRON MAN'S...
...BUT BIGGER. A *LOT* BIGGER. AND WITH MORE WEAPONS.

THE SOVIETS WERE OUR ALLIES AGAINST HYDRA...DID THINGS CHANGE THAT MUCH SINCE I WAS FROZEN?
UM, YES. A LOT. IT'S...COMPLICATED. BUT VANKO ISN'T. HE'S OBSESSED WITH DESTROYING IRON MAN. HIS ARMOR IS BASED ON TONY'S TECH...
...AND TONY, WELL...LET'S JUST SAY HE'S A LITTLE PROTECTIVE OF HIS TECHNOLOGY.

IRON MAN HAS BEEN TRYING TO TAKE VANKO DOWN EVER SINCE THEY FIRST MET...AND HE FINALLY DID.

UNTIL THE BREAKOUT.
RIGHT. WE'RE TRACKING ALL THE ESCAPED VILLAINS, BUT I'M PRETTY SURE THIS ONE'S AT THE TOP OF IRON MAN'S LIST.
SOMETIMES I FORGET WHO IS OBSESSED WITH WHOM.
YOU SAID THIS 'VANKO' HAD WEAPONS?

YES, A LOT. WHY DO YOU--
AH. NEVERMIND.
IF I HAD TO GUESS...

...I'D SAY IRON MAN'S FOUND THE CRIMSON DYNAMO.
OBSESSION
POUR IT ON, AVENGERS!
WHATEVER IT TAKES, JUST PUT HIM DOWN!!

YOU ARE A COWARD, IRON MAN! DO YOU HEAR ME?! A COWARD!
YOU KNEW I WOULD DESTROY YOU DURING THE BREAKOUT, SO YOU RAN! AND NOW YOU BRING OTHERS TO FIGHT FOR YOU!

TRULY, IRON MAN, THIS DYNAMO TALKS TOO MUCH.
WARNING... EXTERNAL SENSORS OFF-LINE!
WELL, FEEL FREE TO SHUT HIM UP, THOR.

HAVE AT THEE, VILLAIN!
KRA-KOOOOOOM!

SO LET ME GET THIS STRAIGHT, YOU'RE A SECOND-RATE IRON MAN KNOCK-OFF WHO REALLY LIKES THE COLOR RED.
THIS IS WHY I'M NOT SKIING THE SWISS ALPS RIGHT NOW?
ZAP!
ZAP!
ZAP!
NO...NOT KNOCKOFF. MY ARMOR IS SUPERIOR. ALLOW ME TO DEMONSTRATE.

AAAH!
KA-THOOOM!
UHN!!

BACK OFF 'COMRADE!'
UHNN!
STAY DOWN, VANKO...

...IT'S OVER. YOU'RE DONE.

YOU STEAL MY TECH, THIS IS WHAT HAPPENS. YOU'RE GOING AWAY FOR A LONG--
TONY...
HE NEEDS TO KNOW, HANK. THEY ALL NEED TO KNOW, MY ARMOR WILL NOT BE USED TO--
IRON MAN...
TONY, JUST TURN AROUND!

TITANIUM MAN!

THE WINTER GUARD HAS COME FOR THE CRIMSON DYNAMO!

DARKSTAR!

...OH.

URSA MAJOR!

VANGUARD!

WHO ARE YOU?! IF YOU'RE WORKING WITH DYNAMO--
WHAT DO YOU WANT WITH DYNAMO?
WE ARE NOT, IRON MAN. I AM CALLED VANGUARD, AND MY TEAM AND I ARE SERVANTS OF THE RUSSIAN FEDERATION.


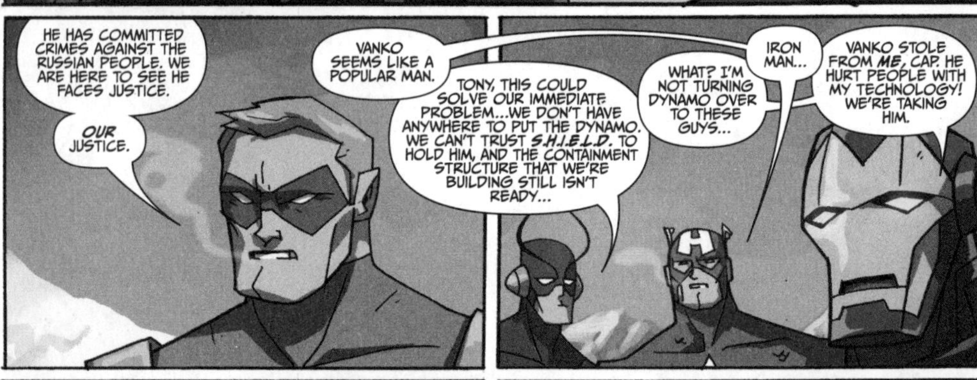

HE HAS COMMITTED CRIMES AGAINST THE RUSSIAN PEOPLE. WE ARE HERE TO SEE HE FACES JUSTICE.
OUR JUSTICE.
VANKO SEEMS LIKE A POPULAR MAN.
TONY, THIS COULD SOLVE OUR IMMEDIATE PROBLEM...WE DON'T HAVE ANYWHERE TO PUT THE DYNAMO. WE CAN'T TRUST S.H.I.E.L.D. TO HOLD HIM, AND THE CONTAINMENT STRUCTURE THAT WE'RE BUILDING STILL ISN'T READY...
IRON MAN...
WHAT? I'M NOT TURNING DYNAMO OVER TO THESE GUYS...
VANKO STOLE FROM ME, CAP. HE HURT PEOPLE WITH MY TECHNOLOGY! WE'RE TAKING HIM.

THEY'VE GOT A BEAR. THAT'S FREAKY.
VERILY.

WE ARE NOT ASKING, IRON MAN. THIS IS GOING TO HAPPEN.
THE WINTER GUARD IS HERE WITH THE PERMISSION OF THE SWISS GOVERNMENT. ARE YOU? BY WHAT AUTHORITY DO YOU TAKE IVAN VANKO?

STEP AWAY FROM THE DYNAMO, AVENGER. WE DO NOT WISH FOR A PROBLEM.
YOU DON'T WISH FOR A PROBLEM? WELL, GUESS WHAT...

WINTER GUARD, ATTACK!
IRON MAN?!
...YOU GOT ONE!!

JARVIS, ANALYZE THAT ARMOR'S SYSTEMS!
UNABLE TO COMPLY. EXTERNAL SENSORS STILL OFF-LINE.
YOUR WEAPONS ARE IMPRESSIVE, MORTAL... BUT ALLOW ME TO SHOW YOU THE POWER OF A TRUE HAMMER!!

WALK AWAY, CAPTAIN...BEFORE YOU AND YOUR TEAMMATES ARE HURT. OR WORSE.
KSHINK!
?!
TALKING BEARS...THE FUTURE GETS WEIRDER EVERY DAY.

YOU CHOSE THIS, AVENGERS... NOT US!
AAAAAHH!
JAN!!

ARE YOU INSANE, IRON MAN? WE BOTH WANT THE SAME THING... CRIMSON DYNAMO IN PRISON!
IS THAT RIGHT? WELL, HERE'S A QUESTION FOR YOU... WHERE'D YOU GET THAT ARMOR?
BECAUSE I CAN'T HELP BUT NOTICE SOME SIMILARITIES TO THE DYNAMO'S... AND THAT MEANS THAT IT'S MINE.
NO... NO! STAY AWAY!
UGH! WHAT IS THAT? IT'S LIKE I WAS STUCK INSIDE THE COLOR BLACK!
AMAZING?! IT TRIED TO EAT ME!
SHE'S MANIPULATING SOME KIND OF ENERGY... IT MIGHT BE OTHER-DIMENSIONAL...THAT'S AMAZING!
TALK TO ME JARVIS...I NEED TO KNOW WHAT'S IN THAT ARMOR...
SENSORS STILL OFF-LINE...
STOP THIS! WE DO NOT WISH TO FIGHT!
YOUR ARMORED WARRIOR WISHES TO STOP THE BATTLE?
WE DID NOT COME HERE TO BATTLE THE AVENGERS. YOUR IRON MAN ATTACKED US.
BUT IF YOU WISH TO FIGHT, WE WILL OBLIGE YOU!

AND THAT'S FOR BLASTING ME WITH YOUR WEIRD BLACK STUFF!!
CAP! THOR! THIS IS POINTLESS! WE'RE THE PROBLEM HERE, NOT THEM!
ZAP!
AAH!

YOUR ANT-MAN SPEAKS THE TRUTH, CAPTAIN...
...IRON MAN. WE NEED TO STAND DOWN.

YOU'RE RIGHT TO SUSPECT THEM, STARK.
WHO DO YOU THINK THEIR FIRST RECRUIT WAS FOR THEIR WINTER GUARD? WHO DO YOU THINK DESIGNED THE TITANIUM MAN ARMOR?

DYNAMO...
HE LIES. YOU CANNOT LISTEN TO HIM...

IRON MAN, THE DYNAMO IS A VILLAIN AND CANNOT BE TRUSTED. HE IS MANIPULATING YOU!

IRON MAN... THEY'RE WILLING TO TALK. LET'S LISTEN TO WHAT THEY HAVE TO SAY.
CAREFULLY.

AND IF WE DON'T LIKE WHAT YOU'VE GOT TO SAY...ZAPPING WILL RESUME.
JAN... THAT'S NOT HELPING.
IRON MAN... I KNOW WHAT'S GOING THROUGH YOUR HEAD. THESE PEOPLE ARE NOT THE ENEMY.

AND WHAT IF YOU'RE WRONG, HANK?
YOU DON'T KNOW WHAT MY TECH CAN DO IN THE WRONG HANDS. I DO. I'VE SEEN IT.

I SENSE NO TRICKERY HERE, IRON MAN.
THE WINTER GUARD ARE FORMIDABLE, AND WHILE THEIR TONE IS FILLED WITH ARROGANCE...
...THE TRUTH IS THAT YOU DID ATTACK FIRST. LET'S TALK TO THEM.

YEAH... WE COULD DO THAT...

...OR I COULD JUST TAKE MY ARMOR BACK AND *THEN* TALK IT OUT!
HAHAHAHAHA!!

WATCH OUT!
BOOOOM!
UHNN!
NO!!

VILLAIN!
PERHAPS. BUT I AM NOT A THIEF, OR A LIAR. NOT LIKE *STARK*.

I'VE GOT YOU!!
UHNNN...

YOU SAVED ME...WHY? WHY WOULD YOU--
YOUR ARMOR...


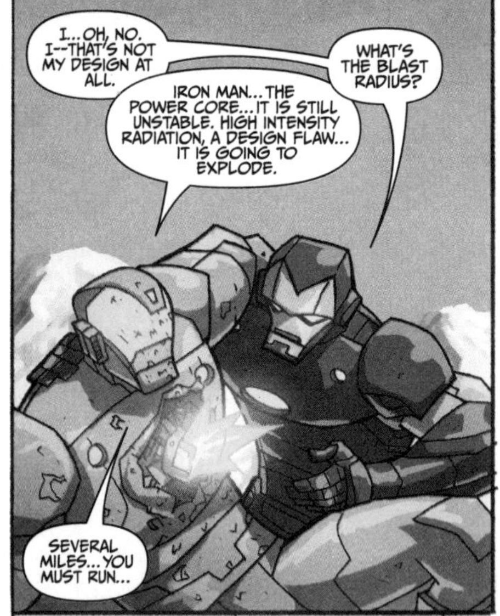

I...OH, NO. I--THAT'S NOT MY DESIGN AT ALL.
IRON MAN...THE POWER CORE...IT IS STILL UNSTABLE. HIGH INTENSITY RADIATION, A DESIGN FLAW... IT IS GOING TO EXPLODE.
WHAT'S THE BLAST RADIUS?
SEVERAL MILES...YOU MUST RUN...

CHUNK!
I DON'T THINK SO.

KRA-KOOOOOM!
SORRY... AVENGERS... MAY HAVE BEEN...
...MAY HAVE BEEN... WRONG...

UHNNN... BEING DEAD... HURTS.

I THINK HE'S OKAY.
WHERE'S DYNAMO?
HE ESCAPED DURING THE EXPLOSION.
IT WAS *REALLY* BIG.

LOOK, VANGUARD...I'M SORRY. THIS IS ALL MY FAULT.
YOU ARE RIGHT.
BUT WE WERE NOT ENTIRELY TRUTHFUL...THE WINTER GUARD DID TRY AND RECRUIT THE DYNAMO. WE REALIZED OUR MISTAKE QUICKLY. BUT NOT BEFORE PEOPLE WERE HURT.
NOW WE TRY TO MAKE UP FOR THAT MISTAKE.

WHEN NEXT WE MEET...LET US MEET AS ALLIES.
AGREED.

GUYS...I'M SORRY. DYNAMO... I GOT BLINDED. I JUST HAD TO BE THE ONE TO TAKE HIM DOWN.
OF COURSE. FOR ALL YOUR GOLD AND SCIENCE, YOU ARE A WARRIOR AT HEART.
IT'S JUST... I'VE SEEN MY TECHNOLOGY DESTROY LIVES TOO OFTEN. SOME-TIMES, I GET OVERWHELMED BY IT.
UNDER-STANDABLE. BUT YOU'RE NOT UP AGAINST THIS ALONE.

I KNOW. IT'S JUST...IT TAKES A LOT OF GETTING USED TO. THIS 'TEAM' THING.
AND NOW, BECAUSE OF ME, CRIMSON DYNAMO IS STILL ON THE LOOSE...

THE NORTHERN COAST OF GERMANY.
STAAAAAARK!!

I WILL MAKE MY ARMOR BETTER... MORE POWERFUL. I WILL DESTROY HIM.
I WILL DESTROY HIM, EVEN IF I HAVE TO DESTROY THE AVENGERS TO DO IT.

CRIMSON DYNAMO!
SHTO?

YOU WISH TO DESTROY THE AVENGERS?
WE CAN HELP.

ONLY THE BEGINNING!

ROOOOAAARRR!
HULK, NO!!
MUTUAL RESPECT

CHOOOM!
HULK, STOP! WE HAVE TO THINK THIS THROUGH!
YOU THINK TOO MUCH. SOMETIMES, YOU JUST NEED TO SMASH.
YOU SHOULD LISTEN TO YOUR GAMMA IRRADIATED FRIEND, GIANT-MAN.
THINKER! WHAT ARE YOU DOING?
WHAT DO YOU WANT?
ISN'T IT OBVIOUS?

WHAM!
HNNN!
I'VE COME TO DESTROY THE AVENGERS, STARTING WITH THE HULK.
YOU SEE, THEY CALL ME THE MAD THINKER.
THIS WOULD BE THE 'MAD' PART.
ENOUGH TALK!
TURN INTO GIANT-MAN AND SHUT HIM UP!
LOOK AT HIM, GIANT-MAN. THE HULK GROWS STRONGER THE ANGRIER HE GETS, THEY SAY.
BUT MERE STRENGTH IS NOTHING AGAINST MY AWESOME ANDROID. IT WILL USE THE HULK'S STRENGTH *AGAINST* HIM. AND DESPITE ALL HIS RAGE...
...THE HULK WILL *FALL*.
WHOOOSSSSSSH!

HRR...
GONNA... TEAR... YOU... APART! HULK SMA--
THOOM!
I BELIEVE HE WAS GOING TO SAY 'SMASH,' DON'T YOU THINK, QUASIMODO?
PROBABILITY 99.9%
WHAT NOW, GIANT-MAN? DID YOU THINK YOU WOULD FIND THE ESCAPED PRISONERS FROM THE BREAKOUT ONE BY ONE AND CONVINCE THEM TO RETURN TO PRISON?
AWAITING ANALYSIS...
WAITING...
DID YOU BELIEVE THE AVENGERS WERE GOING TO REASON WITH SOME OF THE MOST VIOLENT BEINGS ON THE PLANET?
FIGHTING, VIOLENCE... THEY CAN'T BE THE SOLUTION. THERE HAS TO BE A BETTER WAY.
THERE'S NOTHING YOU CAN DO TO STOP IT, GIANT-MAN. THE HULK IS FINISHED.
RRRRAAAA!!!
THUMP!

YOU'RE WEAK, PYM! LIKE PUNY BANNER!
ALL THAT MATTERS IS STRENGTH!
AND HULK...IS STRONGEST...
...THERE IS!!
NO. SOMETHING'S WRONG. THIS ISN'T ABOUT STRENGTH. IT'S NOT ABOUT DESTROYING THE AVENGERS...
WHAT DOES HE WANT? THINK...
HULK! UNDER THE ARM, THERE'S A NERVE CLUSTER! HIT IT!!

RAAAAA!!!
VZZT!
VZZT!
VT! VT!
HMM. IMPRESSIVE OBSERVATIONAL SKILLS.
IT WOULD HAVE BEEN SO MUCH EASIER TO TRANSFORM INTO GIANT-MAN AND STOP ALL THIS.
BUT THAT'S EXACTLY WHAT YOU WANTED, WASN'T IT? YOU PUT ME IN THIS SITUATION, YOU KEPT CALLING ME GIANT-MAN, EVEN THOUGH I WAS ANT-SIZED...
TELL ME, THINKER...WHAT WOULD HAVE HAPPENED IF I HAD TRANSFORMED TO GIANT-MAN IN FRONT OF YOU?
I'VE BEEN INTRIGUED BY YOUR 'PYM PARTICLES' FOR SOME TIME. I DESIGNED QUASIMODO HERE TO ANALYZE AND REPLICATE ENERGY.
ONCE I UNLOCKED THE PARTICLES' SECRETS...

...WELL, WHAT WOULD HAPPEN THEN IS ANYBODY'S GUESS.
FASCINATING. YOUR ABILITY TO CONTROL INSECTS SEEMED SO... INSIGNIFICANT.
SO INSIGNIFI-- ZZKKQUARK!!
ALL THIS... TO FIGURE OUT HOW YOU GROW?
THE MAD THINKER DOESN'T CARE ABOUT DESTROYING THE AVENGERS, OR TAKING OVER THE WORLD. ALL HE CARES ABOUT IS OBTAINING KNOWLEDGE, NO MATTER WHAT.
IF I HAD FOUGHT... HE WOULD HAVE WON.
HUH. MAYBE YOU'RE NOT AS WEAK AS I THOUGHT.
THANKS.
I SAID 'MAYBE.'
END.

3

YOU'VE FOUND SOMETHING HERE? THIS PLANET IS PRIMITIVE...THE CREATURES LOOK LIKE THEY'VE JUST RISEN FROM THE MUD.
YOU'D BE SURPRISED. THERE IS POWER ON THIS PLANET...THEY CALL IT 'EARTH.'
...WHICH TRANSLATES AS 'DIRT.' LOVELY. WHAT KIND OF CREATURE IS IT?
A MONSTER THEY CALL THE HULK.
A SAVAGE THE LIKES OF WHICH THE UNIVERSE HAS NEVER SEEN.

AND THIS 'HULK,' HE RULES HERE?
NO...IT ISN'T INTERESTED IN RULING, IT ONLY WISHES TO BE LEFT ALONE. OTHER POWERS ON THE PLANET HAVE TRIED TO CONTAIN IT, BUT HAVE FAILED... EVEN AN ASGARDIAN.
REALLY...AN ASGARDIAN, HERE? YOUR HULK MUST BE POWERFUL INDEED TO HAVE BESTED ONE OF ODIN'S ILK.
THE CONTEST WAS... INCONCLUSIVE.

SAVAGE
THE HULK'S RAGE IS...IMPRESSIVE.
I BELIEVE IT TO BE THE MORE POWERFUL OF THE TWO.

WELL THEN, COLLECTOR... I PROPOSE A WAGER.
YOUR HULK AGAINST THE ASGARDIAN.
I WON'T PLAY YOUR GAMES, GRANDMASTER. THE HULK WILL BE PART OF MY COLLECTION. AND BESIDES, YOU HAVE NOTHING I WANT.
AH, BUT YOU HAVEN'T HEARD THE STAKES YET.
IF YOUR MONSTER WINS, MY INFINITY GEM IS YOURS. IF THE ASGARDIAN WINS, YOUR GEM IS MINE TO TAKE.

NO ELDER OF THE UNIVERSE HAS EVER HELD *TWO* OF THE INFINITY GEMS... THE POWER THEY CONTAIN...
I ACCEPT.

THEN LET THE GAMES BEGIN.

SOMEWHERE OVER NORTHERN CANADA.
WHEN WE FIND HIM, THOR, YOU HAVE TO PROMISE ME...YOU'RE NOT GOING TO HIT HIM.
I CANNOT PROMISE THAT. HE PROVOKED ME.
ARE YOU SERIOUS?!

I TAKE IT THOR AND THE HULK DO NOT GET ALONG.
WASP, WHAT EXACTLY CAUSED THE HULK TO LEAVE THE AVENGERS?
OH, YOU KNOW, HULK GOT CRANKY, THOR LIKES TO FIGHT... THINGS HAPPENED.
PLUS, THIS ASGARDIAN WITCH NAMED THE ENCHANTRESS KIND OF SORT OF PUT A MAGIC SPELL ON THE HULK THAT MADE HIM GO NUTS.
...I SEE.

LOOK, WE HAVE TO CONVINCE HIM TO COME BACK WITH US. THE HULK ALREADY THINKS WE DON'T TRUST HIM, WE CAN'T JUST GO IN AND START A FIGHT.
I DO NOT START FIGHTS. I END THEM.
THAT'S NOT HELPING, THOR.

FINE. I SWEAR I WILL NOT ATTACK THE HULK. UNLESS HE PROVOKES--
--HT!!
THOR? ARE YOU--

KRAKOOOOM!

SEVERAL MILES AWAY...
DO YOU FEEL BETTER NOW?
DO YOU THINK THAT UNLEASHING ALL YOUR ANGER ON TREES AND ROCKS IS GOING TO HELP US?
GO AWAY.
YOU KNOW I CAN'T DO THAT.
WE'RE THE SAME. WE'RE IN THIS TOGETHER.
AND I'M TELLING YOU, YOU HAVE TO GO BACK TO THE AVENGERS.
NOT GONNA HAPPEN. THEY THINK I'M A MONSTER. THEY'RE RIGHT.
YOU DON'T HAVE TO BE. YOU CAN BE A HERO, JUST LIKE THEM.
THEY DON'T TRUST ME.
IT WAS A MISTAKE. IT WASN'T YOU.
LISTENING TO *YOU* WAS A MISTAKE!
I DON'T NEED YOU, I DON'T NEED ANYBODY!
I JUST WANT TO BE LEFT ALONE!!
I DON'T THINK THAT'S GOING TO HAPPEN.

CHOOM!

HURR... HURR...
GONNA TEAR... GONNA TEAR YOU APART...
DO YOU HEAR ME, BLONDIE? I'M GONNA TAKE THAT HAMMER AND--

SOMETHING'S WRONG. SOMETHING'S WRONG WITH THOR...
DON'T CARE. KNOW WHY?

HULK SMASH!!

REBOOT IN PROGRESS.
WHAT HAPPENED?!
IT WOULD APPEAR THAT THOR CALLED DOWN A LIGHTNING BOLT ON BOTH YOU AND THE QUINJET.
THANKS, THAT PART I GOT. IS EVERYBODY OKAY?
WE'RE GOOD! GIANT MAN CAUGHT US. I'VE NEVER BEEN STRUCK BY LIGHTNING BEFORE!
YOUR QUINJETS ARE DESIGNED PRETTY WELL, IRON MAN. I THINK IT'S REBOOTING NOW.
THOR FLEW OFF THAT WAY. WHAT HAPPENED?
THAT'S WHAT I ASKED...
IF THOR WAS INTENT ON ATTACKING THE HULK, I SUSPECT HE HAS FOUND HIM.
WOW, THAT'S A LOT...WAIT.
THOR'S OUT THERE, BUT THERE'S SOMETHING ELSE.
TWO SOMETHINGS, ACTUALLY...SOME KIND OF POWER I'VE NEVER SEEN BEFORE.
WHY CAN'T ANYTHING EVER BE EASY?
IT WOULD SEEM YOU FIND IT EASY TO COMPLAIN.
SIGH
YOU KNOW, YOU'RE STILL ON PROBATIONARY STATUS, PANTHER.

RRRAAAAAA!!!...
I FEAR YOU'VE MADE A POOR CHOICE, GRANDMASTER. YOUR OBSESSION WITH GAMES WILL BE YOUR UNDOING.
AND YOUR EXCITEMENT OVER COLLECTING EVERY NEW MONSTER YOU FIND WILL BE YOURS.
LOOK AT THE HULK...HE IS RAGE INCARNATE.

YOUR MINDLESS BRUTE IS POWERFUL, BUT I WAS SURPRISED THAT YOU DID NOT RECOGNIZE HIS FOE, BEING SUCH AN AVID COLLECTOR...
THAT IS NO MERE ASGARDIAN... THAT IS THE SON OF ODIN HIMSELF. THAT IS *THOR*.

AH, BUT YOU MISUNDERSTAND... THE HULK'S POWER IS NOT THAT OF ANY MERE MORTAL.
YOU SEE, WHAT I LEARNED WATCHING HIM WAS THAT THE ANGRIER THE HULK GETS...

...THE STRONGER HE GETS.

AND GIVEN THE HULK'S RAGE, AND THUS HIS STRENGTH... THEY HAVE NO LIMIT.

NO MATTER HIS SKILL OR POWER, THE ASGARDIAN WILL FALL TO MY SAVAGE.
I THINK NOT...FOR YOUR MINDLESS MONSTER IS ABOUT TO LEARN THE MEANING OF TRUE POWER.
CHOOM!

HR?

YOU SAW THEM...UP THERE, WATCHING...THEY MUST BE MAKING THOR DO THIS! YOU HAVE TO TALK TO HIM, GET HIM TO STOP!
YOU WANT ME TO TALK TO HIM?! HE'S ABOUT TO TAKE MY HEAD OFF!
WE HAVE TO HELP HIM!

LIKE HE HELPED ME? I DON'T THINK SO. IT'S HIM OR US.
IT DOESN'T HAVE TO BE THAT WAY. THOR'S BEING USED, JUST LIKE EVERYONE TRIES TO USE YOU.
YOU CAN SAVE HIM. YOU DECIDE WHO YOU ARE, NOT ANYONE ELSE.

...FINE.

WHAT IS HE DOING?
I THINK YOUR SAVAGE IS TRYING TO *THINK*.
*HEY! YOU TWO!*
*YOU'VE GOT SOME EXPLAINING TO DO.*
YEAH! STARTING WITH WHAT *ARE* YOU?
HNN!!
YOU'RE BEING CONTROLLED! YOU CAN *FIGHT* IT!
UNLESS YOU'RE *WEAK* LIKE *BANNER!*
SO *FIGHT!* OR JUST LET THEM *USE* YOU. LET THEM TURN YOU INTO A WEAPON, MAKE YOU *HURT* PEOPLE.
BECAUSE THAT'S WHAT THEY'LL DO. I KNOW.
YOU LIKE TO FIGHT? SO FIGHT NOW!
I, UH, DON'T THINK THIS IS WORKING. I THINK WE NEED A NEW PLAN.
IF HE'S IN THERE, HE WON'T DO IT. HE WON'T HIT YOU.
HE'S HIT YOU BEFORE, I DON'T--WAIT. DID YOU SAY *ME?*
YEAH.

YOU.
OH, NO. HULK...I MEAN, BRUCE...THOR'S GOING TO--
WHATEVER YOU TWO ARE DOING TO THOR, STOP IT RIGHT NOW OR--
I THINK IT'S TRYING TO THREATEN US.
AMUSING.
YES, I--WAIT. THE ASGARDIAN... HE FIGHTS ME...
HNN...
NO... CANNOT...WILL NOT...
THOR WILL NOT BE USED!

UHN!!

YOU KNEW. YOU KNEW HE WOULDN'T DO IT.
HMPH. NOT REALLY. JUST DIDN'T CARE IF HE DID.

YOU DARE INVADE MY MIND, BLUE MAN? YOU WILL PAY FOR SUCH AN INTRUSION!
YOU'RE SURROUNDED, SO MAKE THIS EASY ON YOURSELVES. SURRENDER.
LITTLE HUMAN, YOU ADDRESS BEINGS OLDER THAN YOUR WORLD. OLDER THAN YOUR SUN.

WE ARE ELDERS OF THE UNIVERSE, AND YOU ARE BUT AN AMUSEMENT. YOUR EXISTENCE MERELY PASSES THE TIME FOR US.
AND IF YOU BEGIN TO BORE US... THEN THERE'S REALLY NO NEED FOR YOU TO EXIST AT ALL.

AVENGERS, ATTACK!

FWASH!!!!...

WHOA! WE DISINTEGRATED THEM!
I THINK THEY TELEPORTED AWAY, WASP. WHO WERE THOSE GUYS?!
I KNOW NOT...BUT THE BLUE ONE WAS INTENT ON MY DESTRUCTION OF THE HULK...WHERE DID--?

THE HULK'S GONE.
I CAN TRACK HIM...

NAY. LET THE HULK GO FOR NOW.
I HAVE TROUBLED HIM ENOUGH THIS DAY, AND HE...HE FOUGHT TO FREE ME FROM THE ELDER'S CONTROL.
NO MATTER HOW HE IS ATTACKED...
...THE HULK REMAINS A HERO.
THE CONTEST IS NOT OVER. HULK, THOR... NO WINNER WAS DETERMINED.
I AGREE. AND THESE AVENGERS... THEY WOULD FIT WELL WITHIN MY COLLECTION.
THIS PLANET COULD INDEED INTEREST THE ELDERS OF THE UNIVERSE.
ALL OF US.
NOT THE END!

IT EATS PEOPLE?! ARE YOU KIDDING ME?!?
COURAGE

WASP...
I MEAN, UH, YOU'RE GOING TO BE FINE, CAP EVERYTHING'S GOING TO BE OKAY. I'M ON THIS!
BUT FOR REAL, YOU KNEW THIS WENDIGO THING ATE PEOPLE WHEN WE CAME OUT HERE?! BECAUSE I DIDN'T KNOW THAT.
IT WAS...IN THE FILE...
I SKIMMED IT! I THOUGHT THIS WAS SOME GUY WITH SOME HAIR ISSUES, MAYBE SOME COLD POWERS...JUST ANOTHER BREAKOUT BAD GUY ON THE LIST. NOT A FULL ON REAL MONSTER.
STORM CAME OUT OF NOWHERE, NO VISIBILITY...WE'RE SITTING DUCKS OUT HERE, AND I'M NO GOOD TO YOU.
WASP, LISTEN TO ME. YOU HAVE TO GO.
WHWEEEEHNHNHOOoooo...
OKAY, THAT'S REALLY CREEPY. YOU'RE RIGHT, I THINK WE NEED TO GET OUT OF--

GRAAAAA!!
WAAAAAA!
EAT HOT BIO-STING, ABOMINABLE SNOWMAN!
HEY! IT'S NOT DOING ANYTHING. IT'S NOT--
OHHHH, NUTS!
WENDIGOOOOO!!
AAAAAHHH!
GET AWAY! GET--
NYEARGHH!
WHAM!!
--AWAY!!

OH MANOH MANOH MAN...
AAOOOOOOOOOOO!!
CAP, COME ON...WE HAVE TO GO, IT'S GOING TO COME BACK. GET UP... YOU HAVE TO GET UP!!
LOST TOO MUCH BLOOD...YOU HAVE TO GO.
CAP, I CAN'T DO THIS ALONE! IT'S OUT THERE, I CAN'T...THERE'S NOTHING I CAN DO AGAINST THAT MONSTER, PLEASE, YOU HAVE TO GET UP!
I'VE SEEN... SEEN YOU FIGHT MONSTERS...
PEOPLE! I FIGHT PEOPLE, AND EVEN THEN I'M SCARED! I'M SCARED ALL THE TIME!
DOESN'T STOP YOU. BEING SCARED... STILL FIGHTING...THAT'S WHAT MAKES YOU BRAVE. WHAT MAKES YOU A HERO.
YOU HAVE TO GO NOW. TAKE MY SHIELD...I'LL HOLD IT OFF...AS LONG AS I CAN.
UHN!
SHUK!
CAP...I'M SORRY.

...HA.
GUESS... YOU'RE GOING TO GET...FROZEN AGAIN, SOLDIER.
...RRRRRR...
MAYBE... NOT...
COME ON, UGLY... COME--

GET AWAY FROM HIM!!
WHAM!

GRRRAAA!!
AAARGH!
OKAY...OKAY... I MAY BE SCARED OUT OF MY MIND OF YOU...
...BUT I'M AN AVENGER!
SHRACK!
AND I'M TAKING YOU DOWN!
DO YOU HEAR ME?!
SHRACK!
SHRACK!
RAAAAAA!!!

CHOOM
CAP... CAP...I DID IT...
CAP, PLEASE BE OKAY...
NEED YOU TO PROMISE...NOT TO TELL THE OTHERS I WAS SCARED. THEY THINK I'M BRAVE.
CAP... PLEASE SAY SOMETHING...
CAP...
...BRAVEST... PERSON...I KNOW...
THANKS, CAP.
...
MAN, I HOPE THIS THING DOESN'T WAKE UP.
END.

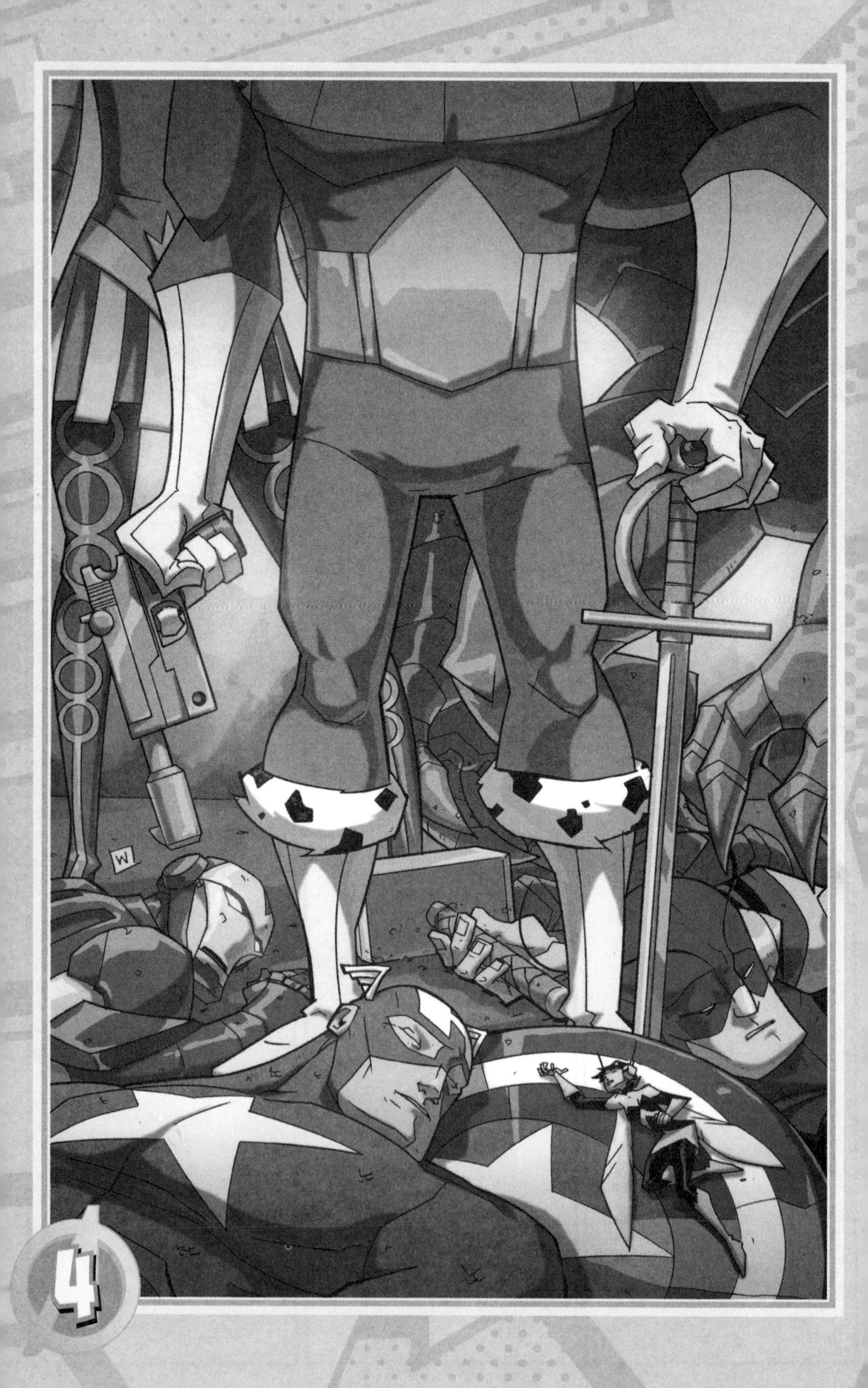
4

LIVE
--INCREDIBLE FOOTAGE COMING IN FROM CALIFORNIA AS IRON MAN SAVES THE CITY...
GIANT ROBOT ATTACKS CITY, IRON MAN SAVES DAY

...FROM WHAT EYEWITNESSES CALL A 'GIANT ROBOT.'
I...I... I...
IRON MAN.

IRON MAN ASSISTED AGENTS OF THE PEACEKEEPING FORCE KNOWN AS S.H.I.E.L.D. IN REMOVAL OF THE ROBOT.
NEITHER IRON MAN NOR S.H.I.E.L.D. WERE AVAILABLE FOR COMMENT, ALTHOUGH IRON MAN DID SIGN AUTOGRAPHS AT THE SCENE.
S.H.I.E.L.D. STORAGE FACILITY OMEGA.

THE APPALACHIAN MOUNTAINS.
THE ORIGINS AND MOTIVES OF THE ROBOT REMAIN UNKNOWN.

SIX MONTHS LATER.
FWASSH!!

BARON ZEMO!
CRIMSON DYNAMO!
WONDER MAN!
EXECUTIONER!
ABOMINATION!
ENCHANTRESS!
WELL, WELL, WELL... WHAT DO WE HAVE HERE?
NOTHING LESS THAN THE DESTRUCTION OF THE AVENGERS.
MY SOURCES WITHIN HYDRA REFER TO IT AS
ULTIMO!
CAN YOU MAKE IT WORK?
YOU MORTALS AND YOUR MACHINES... THIS WILL BE SUITABLE.
OH, YES. I CAN MAKE IT WORK.
I CAN MAKE IT BURN THIS WORLD TO THE GROUND.

AVENGERS MANSION, NEW YORK CITY.
JUST ONE LITTLE TEAM PICTURE!
NO.
OH, COME ON! WHY NOT?!
BECAUSE I'M WORKING? JUST PHOTOSHOP ME IN.
WHAT?!
ISO 400
3
5700K
59% X.FINE
185
I THINK OUR TIME WOULD BE BETTER SERVED TRAINING. KANG'S INVASION WAS--
OKAY, OKAY...
--THE PROPERTIES OF THE PYM PARTICLES ARE STILL UNSTABLE WHEN APPLIED TO OBJECTS SEPARATE FROM--
UGH!
WAIT, PANTHER... WHERE'D YOU GO?
MY UNIFORM IS NOT VISIBLE TO TRADITIONAL ELECTRONICS.
GET THAT OUT OF MY FACE RIGHT NOW.
GEEZ, RELAX!
THIS 'DIGITAL CAMERA' IS YET MORE SOULLESS MORTAL TECHNOLOGY... BETTER TO HAVE A TRUE ARTIST RENDER US...
YOU WANT ME TO DO WHAT?
NEVER MIND.

YOU GUYS STINK.
ARE YOU STILL TRYING TO MAKE THIS PICTURE THING HAPPEN?
YES! I MEAN, SERIOUSLY, IS THIS SO MUCH TO ASK? WE CAN'T HAVE ONE NICE PHOTOGRAPH OF ALL OF US TOGETHER?
YES.

AND WHY EXACTLY DO WE NEED THIS?
BECAUSE WE'RE A TEAM! AND MORE THAN THAT, WE'RE FRIENDS!
YOU'RE CRAZY, YOU KNOW THAT, RIGHT? WE WORK TOGETHER. THAT'S IT.

WHY? WHY DOES THAT HAVE TO BE IT? WHY CAN'T WE HANG OUT AND HAVE FUN EVERY ONCE IN A WHILE, WHY DOES IT HAVE TO BE THAT THE ONLY TIME WE'RE TOGETHER IS WHEN THE WORLD NEEDS SAVING?
AW, MAN!!
RRRRUMMMMBLLE!
YOU KNOW YOU MADE THIS HAPPEN, RIGHT?

OKAY, WHAT IS THAT?!
DOES IT MATTER? OH, BY THE WAY...

THE AVENGERS: EARTH'S MIGHTIEST HEROES IN TEAM
...I QUIT.
NO! I STILL NEED TO GET MY PICTURE!!

THIS ONE MIGHT BE MY FAULT... THAT'S ULTIMO.
AND WHAT EXACTLY IS AN 'ULTIMO'?
YOUR STANDARD GIANT ROBOT. I WAS PRETTY SURE I BLEW HIM UP...
I'D SAY HE GOT BETTER.
ENOUGH TALK...

...TIME TO SMASH!
HULK, WAIT!!
...I THINK I'M GONNA NEED A WIDER LENS.

Okay, not the best shot of the Hulk. But good lighting! PS, he survived.

CHOOOOOM!
AVENGERS ASSEMBLE!!
HAVE AT THEE, ROBOT!!
THOR, WAIT! GET CLOSER TO IRON MAN!
JAN, PUT THAT THING AWAY! THIS IS SERIOUS!
OH, LIKE WE HAVEN'T FOUGHT A GIANT ROBOT BEFORE. WHAT MAKES THIS ANY DIFFERENT THAN--
IRON MAN!!
UHN!!
ZZARRRK!
DESTROY THEM ALL.
BUT CAPTAIN AMERICA IS MINE.

OHHHHH, NUTS.
YOU HAVE GOT TO BE KIDDING ME, DON'T WE HAVE ENOUGH TO CONTEND WITH? DO WE REALLY NEED THE MASTERS OF EVIL, TOO?
LOOK AT THE ROBOT'S EYES... IT IS BEING CONTROLLED BY THE ENCHANT--

WHAM!!
FWOOSH
PANTHER!!

THAT ENERGY IT'S FIRING, I'VE NEVER SEEN ANYTHING LIKE IT... AMAZING.
DO WE HAVE A PLAN HERE?

THOOOM!
I'M GOING TO ENJOY CRUSHING YOU, AVENGER!
IRON MAN! THOR!
YOU TWO CONCENTRATE ON THE ROBOT, THE REST OF US WILL DEAL WITH THE MASTERS!

I THINK ANT-MAN WAS ASKING ME IF WE HAD A PLAN, CAP.
NOT REALLY.
THANKS, HANK.
COME, IRON MAN... LET US SHOW THIS MECHANICAL MAN THAT TECHNOLOGY IS NO MATCH FOR THE AVENGERS!!
...I HATE THIS JOB.

Okay, this was pretty cool, but it's only Tony and Thor. Everyone else was fighting the Masters of Evil. Man! Evil ruins everything.

AVENGERS... LOOK. ULTIMO IS ABSORBING THE ATTACKS.
THE ROBOT IS GROWING WITH EACH STRIKE.

AW, MAN... HE'S RIGHT. THAT THING'S GETTING BIGGER.
DYNAMO'S ON YOUR LEFT.
I SEE HIM. HE'S COVERED.

RRRRAAAAA!
AAAHH!

HAWKEYE, WATCH OUT!!
SSHRRAKKKK!
ARGH!!

THE ARCHER ANNOYED ME.
ARE YOU READY, CAPTAIN? MY SWORD AWAITS YOU.
CAP, WHAT DO WE DO?
WHAT WE ALWAYS DO, WASP.
PICK A TARGET AND TAKE IT DOWN!!

No, for real, I almost died getting this shot.

UHN!!
KRA-KOOOOM!
TRULY, THE MACHINE IS POWERFUL. HOW DID YOU DEFEAT IT WHEN LAST YOU MET, IRON MAN?

I USED AN EMP, THEN BLASTED HIM... BUT I ALREADY TRIED IT. I THINK IT'S ADAPTING.

ANALYZING

ANALYZING

ANALYZING

TARGET ACQUIRED

WHOA!!
THE BLAST...IT WAS NOT DIRECTED TOWARD US...
SCHRAKK!!

BOOM
AAAIIEEEE!!

ZEMO, THE ROBOT... IT--
I SAW, WONDER MAN. THIS CHANGES THINGS.
MASTERS OF EVIL! WE ARE LEAVING!

YEAARGHH!
CHOOM!

IRON MAN! ANT-MAN! WE NEED A WAY TO TAKE THIS THING DOWN!
EVERYTHING WE THROW AT IT JUST GIVES IT MORE POWER...
WHAM! WHAM! WHAM!

ENCHANTRESS AND DYNAMO ARE DOWN. I'M NOT SURE IF THIS IS GOOD OR BAD.
IT IS BAD. THE MASTERS HAVE LOST CONTROL OF ULTIMO.
MAYBE WE SHOULD OFFER IT A SPOT ON OUR TEAM.

THAT'S IT. MORE POWER.
IT MUST HAVE AN UPPER LIMIT. WE CAN OVERLOAD IT...
HANK! WHERE ARE YOU GOING?!
AS MUCH AS I HATE TO SAY IT... VIOLENCE MAY BE THE SOLUTION HERE.

Look at Hank... he's so nerdy but then BOOOM! Giant-Man smackdown. Sigh. I love him.

IRON MAN...
IT'S WORTH A TRY, BUT THINGS WILL GET WORSE BEFORE THEY GET BETTER. WE NEED TO HIT HIM AS HARD AS WE CAN, AS FAST AS WE CAN.
YOU HEARD THE MAN, AVENGERS... OPEN FIRE ON ULTIMO WITH EVERYTHING YOU'VE GOT!
WHAT ABOUT THE MASTERS?

YOUR NECKS ARE ON THE LINE, TOO, ZEMO. WE COULD USE THE EXTRA FIRE-POWER.
SURELY YOU ARE NOT *SERIOUS*, CAPTAIN.
WE NEED TO GET OUT OF HERE, ZEMO!

YOUR RIDE HOME IS STILL UNCONSCIOUS, ZEMO. YOU BETTER HOPE YOU RUN FASTER THAN ULTIMO.

WONDER MAN! WHERE ARE YOU GOING?
YOU SAID IT WOULD TAKE DOWN THE AVENGERS, NOT DESTROY NEW YORK!
I'M GOING TO HELP.

VERY WELL. ABOMINATION, EXECUTIONER...
DESTROY ULTIMO.

STILL WANT A PICTURE?
...YEAH.
WELL, GET READY.

Wow. Just...
Wow.
'Nuff said.

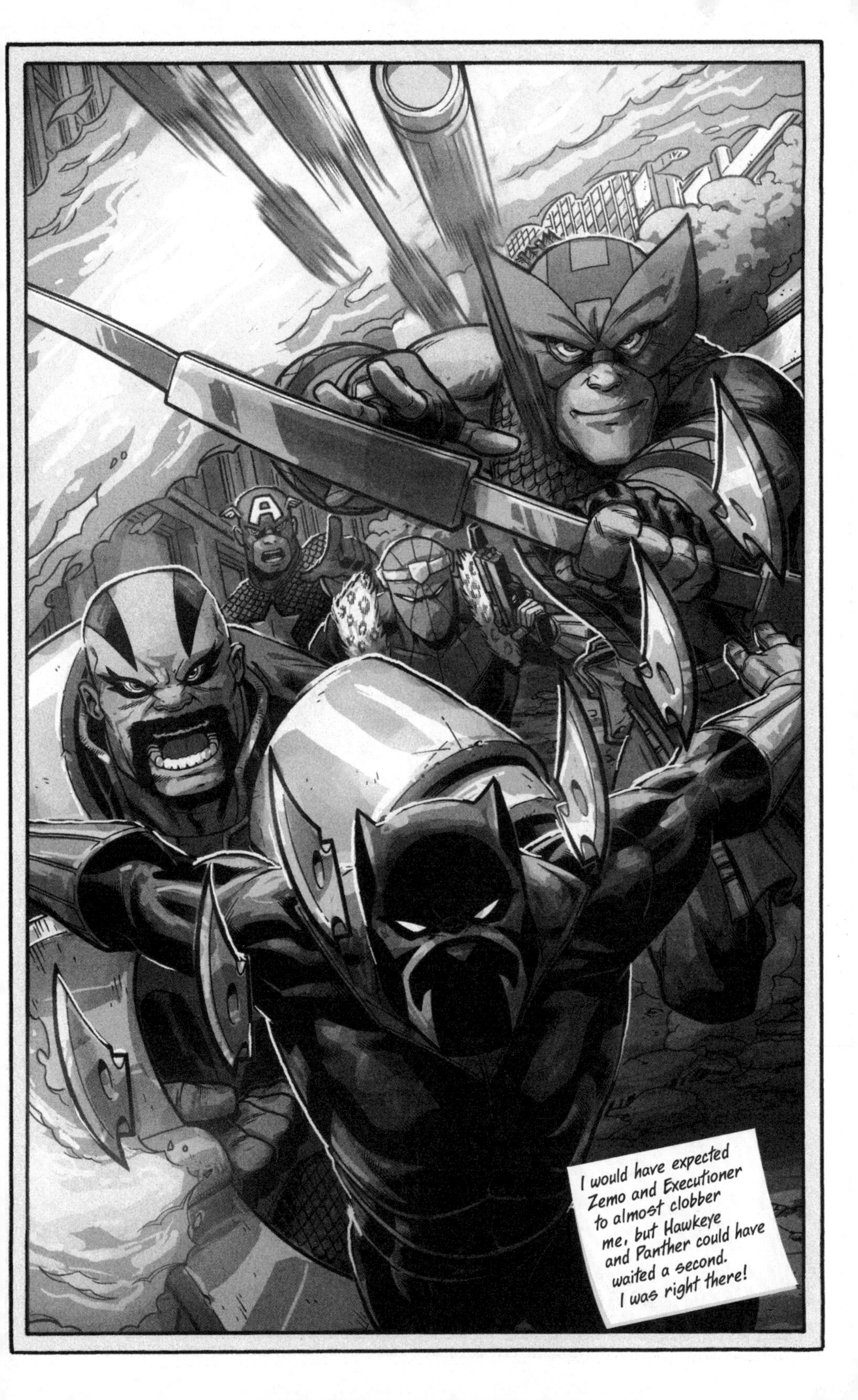
I would have expected
Zemo and Executioner
to almost clobber
me, but Hawkeye
and Panther could have
waited a second.
I was right there!

Big. And it
was really
loud, too.

IT'S WORKING! ULTIMO'S POWER CORE IS OVER-LOADING!
WATCH OUT!! IT'S GOING TO--
KA-KA-KOOOOM!

THOR! THE DEBRIS!
CHOOM!
CHOOM!
CHOOM!
FEAR NOT, IRON MAN!

AAAAAAAND DÉJÀ VU.

SURRENDER, ZEMO. YOU'RE OUTNUMBERED, AND THE ENCHANTRESS IS STILL DOWN.
YOU CAN'T WIN.
AH, BUT YOU SEE, FOR ALL OUR DIFFERENCES, THERE IS ONE THING WE HAVE IN COMMON, CAPTAIN.
NEITHER OF US WILL EVER SURRENDER. THERE IS ONLY ONE WAY THIS CAN END.
...I KNOW.
AVENGERS... TAKE 'EM DOWN.
UHNN... ZEMO, WHAT--
CURSE YOU, MORTALS.
NO!
FWASSH!

WE WON!
THE MASTERS GOT AWAY.
WELL, THE GIANT ROBOT DIDN'T! SO LET'S CELEBRATE!

RATHER FIGHT THE ROBOT MORE.
WASP...
NO! YOU CAN FIGHT IT ALL YOU WANT, BUT WE ARE GOING TO BE FRIENDS, ALL OF US! IT'S INEVITABLE!

WE'VE SAVED THE WORLD LIKE A HUNDRED TIMES NOW, WE'VE BEEN THROUGH HORRIBLE THINGS, WE'VE SAVED EACH OTHER'S LIVES!
WE ARE IN THIS TOGETHER, AND IT'S TIME YOU ALL STARTED ACTING LIKE IT!
FINE. MAYBE... MAYBE WE COULD ALL GO GRAB A BITE TO EAT. YOU KNOW. AS A TEAM.

YES!!

BUT FIRST THINGS FIRST.
YOU, KID, WHAT'S YOUR NAME?
PETER. PETER PARKER.
GREAT! CAN YOU TAKE A PICTURE FOR ME?

Finally! A team shot! Was that so hard?!
Because whether they admit it or not, we're a team. We're a family. We're Earth's Mightiest Heroes!!
END.

MARVEL
EARTH'S MIGHTIEST HEROES!
the AVENGERS
DISNEY XD

# CHARACTER PROFILES

## IRON MAN

NAME: TONY STARK

BILLIONAIRE INVENTOR TONY STARK BRINGS HIS MATCHLESS INTELLECT TO LIFE IN HIS GREATEST CREATION – THE INVINCIBLE **IRON MAN** ARMOR! CAPABLE OF BLASTING REPULSOR RAYS AT MACH 10 AND WITHSTANDING HEAVY ARMS FIRE, IRON MAN VIGILANTLY SEEKS TO RID THE WORLD OF CORRUPTION. BUT AS GLOBAL THREATS ESCALATE BEYOND EVEN IRON MAN'S CAPACITY, HE MUST ASSEMBLE THE GREATEST SUPER HERO TEAM IN HISTORY... **THE AVENGERS!**

CAPTAIN AMERICA
NAME: STEVE ROGERS
DURING WORLD WAR II, STEVE ROGERS FOUGHT TYRANNY AS CAPTAIN AMERICA USING HIS SERUM-ENHANCED STRENGTH AND VIBRANIUM SHIELD TO PROTECT THE FREE WORLD! BUT A NOBLE SACRIFICE LEFT THE SUPER SOLDIER FROZEN IN ICE FOR DECADES, AND NOW CAPTAIN AMERICA FINDS HIMSELF STRUGGLING TO FIT INTO THE MODERN WORLD. FORTUNATELY, CAP'S PAST HEROICS HAVE INSPIRED A NEW GENERATION OF HEROES WHO SHARE HIS OLD-FASHIONED VALUES...THE AVENGERS!

CHARACTER PROFILES
THOR
Renowned as the strongest warrior in all of the Nine Realms, THOR was deeply moved by the nobility of "mere mortals" on Earth. And so, wielding his mythic hammer Mjolnir, the legendary champion loyally defends man's world. But when the Thunderer's elemental might isn't enough to turn the tide, Thor looks to his heroic comrades-in-arms...
THE AVENGERS!

HULK
NAME: BRUCE BANNER
HIGH LEVELS OF GAMMA RADIATION RELEASED THE SHORT-TEMPERED BEHEMOTH TRAPPED INSIDE SCIENTIST BRUCE BANNER ...THE INCREDIBLE HULK! SINCE HE FIRST SURFACED, COUNTLESS MILITARY AGENCIES HAVE PURSUED THE HULK AS A MONSTER, FAILING TO SEE THAT THE SUPER-STRONG JADE GIANT FOLLOWS A SIMPLE, BUT NOBLE, MORAL COMPASS. HULK HOPES TO PROVE THAT THERE TRULY IS A HEROIC HEART BENEATH HIS RAMPAGING EXTERIOR, BY JOINING THE WORLD'S PREEMINENT SUPER-TEAM...THE AVENGERS!

# CHARACTER PROFILES

## WASP

### NAME: JANET VAN DYNE

THE WINSOME JANET VAN DYNE DITCHED HER SHALLOW LIFE AS A SOCIALITE, HOPING TO DO MORE TO BENEFIT MANKIND. REDUCING HERSELF TO INSECT SIZE AND SPROUTING BIO-ORGANIC WINGS, SHE SATISFIES HER NEED FOR JUSTICE AND ADVENTURE AS THE **WASP!** NATURALLY, WHEN THE WINGED WONDER LEARNED THAT EARTH'S MIGHTIEST HEROES WERE GATHERING TOGETHER, WASP GLADLY CONTRIBUTED HER ELECTRIC STING TO...**THE AVENGERS!**

## ANT-MAN

### A.K.A. GIANT MAN
### NAME: HANK PYM

HIS ASTONISHING "PYM PARTICLES" ALLOWED MICROBIOLOGIST HANK PYM TO EXPLORE THE QUANTUM WORLD IN WAYS HE NEVER IMAGINED! ALSO OUTFITTED WITH A CYBERNETIC HELMET THAT ALLOWS HIM TO COMMUNICATE WITH INSECTS, PYM CAN SHRINK TO SUBATOMIC SCALE AS **ANT-MAN!** THOUGH SOMEWHAT OUT OF HIS LEAGUE WORKING ALONGSIDE THE MOST POWERFUL BEINGS ON THE PLANET, ANT-MAN OFTEN PROVIDES A GROUNDED PERSPECTIVE FOR EARTH'S MIGHTIEST HEROES...
**THE AVENGERS!**

HAWKEYE
NAME: CLINT BARTON
TRAINED BY S.H.I.E.L.D. TO BE AN EXPERT SHARPSHOOTER, THE HOTDOGGING CLINT BARTON PREFERS TO SHOW OFF HIS KEEN MARKSMANSHIP SKILLS WITH A SIMPLE BOW. ARMED WITH AN ARRAY OF HIGH-TECH ARROWS, THE REBELLIOUS HAWKEYE OFTEN GOES TO GREAT LENGTHS TO DEMONSTRATE THAT HIS TALENTS AND TRICK ARROWS DESERVE A PLACE AMONG THE EARTH'S MIGHTIEST HEROES. AND WHILE HIS ATTITUDE AND FAST TALK OFTEN GET HIM INTO TROUBLE WITH HIS TEAMMATES, HAWKEYE HAS NONETHELESS PROVED HIMSELF AN INVALUABLE MEMBER OF... THE AVENGERS!
THE BLACK PANTHER
NAME: T'CHALLA
DESPITE A BRILLIANT TACTICAL MIND AND A STOCKPILE OF VIBRANIUM WEAPONS, THE REVERED WARRIOR-KING T'CHALLA WAS OUSTED FROM HIS WAKANDAN THRONE. SECRETIVE AND SUSPICIOUS BY NATURE, THE PROUD T'CHALLA DOESN'T COME BY ALLIES EASILY. AND YET TO END HIS EXILE AND BRING REFORM TO HIS HOMELAND, THE BLACK PANTHER MUST PAIR HIS ENHANCED STRENGTH AND SENSES WITH THE ONLY ONES WHO CAN HELP HIM RECLAIM HIS KINGDOM...THE AVENGERS!

# CHARACTER PROFILES

## NICK FURY

A master tactician and an unrivaled soldier, **DIRECTOR NICK FURY** has lived for years in the gray areas between law and order. Taking after his father, Sgt. Jack Fury, who once dominated the battlefields of **WWII** with an elite military ops squad called the "Howling Commandos", Nick has shown an impressive command of the field and knack for leadership.

As head of The Strategic Homeland Intervention, Enforcement, and Logistics Division – or **S.H.I.E.L.D.** – Fury handles the tough calls that no one else has the guts to make. Unimpressed by super-powered heroes like the **AVENGERS**, Fury prefers to hedge his bets on intense preparation, old-school espionage, and high-tech firepower.

BLACK WIDOW
NAME: NATASHA ROMANOFF
ORIGINALLY A RUSSIAN AGENT, NATASHA EVENTUALLY ENLISTED WITH S.H.I.E.L.D. UNDER THE COMMAND OF DIRECTOR NICK FURY. ALONGSIDE PARTNER AND FELLOW AGENT CLINT BARTON, A.K.A. HAWKEYE, SHE HELD THE JOINT COMMAND OF S.H.I.E.L.D.'S MOST ELITE SPECIAL OPS TEAM.
AN AGENT WITH MATCHLESS TACTICAL EXPERTISE AND COMBAT TRAINING, THE BLACK WIDOW IS ONE OF THE PREMIER HAND-TO-HAND COMBATANTS IN THE WORLD. HER TRUE ALIGNMENT REMAINS MYSTERIOUS, HOWEVER, AS HER TIES TO THE VILLAINOUS ORGANIZATION KNOWN AS HYDRA HAVE TURNED HER INTO A ROGUE ELEMENT WITHIN S.H.I.E.L.D.

# CHARACTER PROFILES

## BARON ZEMO

### NAME: HEINRICH ZEMO

BARON ZEMO WAS THE HEAD OF HYDRA'S NON-CONVENTIONAL WEAPONS DIVISION DURING WORLD WAR II; RESPONSIBLE FOR THE IMPERFECT HYDRA SERUM THAT CREATED THE RED SKULL, AND WHICH HAS ALSO ALLOWED ZEMO TO SURVIVE OVER THE YEARS. GENETIC ENHANCEMENT, BREEDING PROGRAMS, VIRUSES...ZEMO HAD HIS HAND IN ALL OF IT.

OVER THE YEARS, HE TOOK CONTROL OF HYDRA AND RULED IT WITH AN IRON FIST, CONTINUING HIS PROJECTS AND WORKING TOWARD WORLD DOMINATION. HE'S BRILLIANT, A STRONG LEADER OF MEN, AND HAS AN INDOMITABLE WILL. AND HE'S EVIL.

HIS VILE ACTS WERE INFAMOUS DURING WORLD WAR II. HE USED TO WEAR A MASK TO CONCEAL HIS IDENTITY AND AVOID RETRIBUTION. DURING A FIGHT WITH CAPTAIN AMERICA HOWEVER, ONE OF HIS EXPERIMENTS BACKFIRED AND HIS MASK BECAME PERMANENTLY GRAFTED TO HIS FACE.

WEAPONS MAKER, GENETICIST, SOLDIER...HE'S THE ANTI-IRON MAN, ANT-MAN AND CAPTAIN AMERICA ALL ROLLED INTO ONE.

## KANG

AN ARMORED CONQUEROR FROM THE FAR-FLUNG FUTURE, **KANG** HAS BROUGHT HIS ARMIES BACK IN TIME TO DEFEAT THOSE HE CONSIDERS TO BE HISTORY'S GREATEST VILLAINS — THE **AVENGERS!**

ARMED WITH ADVANCED WEAPONRY FROM THE 40TH CENTURY AND THE SECRETS OF TIME-TRAVEL, KANG HAS COME BACK TO THE 21ST CENTURY TO CORRECT AN ERROR IN THE TIME-STREAM. A MOMENT IN THE AVENGERS' PRESENT DAY HAS CAUSED THE END OF KANG'S FUTURE — AND WITH IT, KANG'S BELOVED PRINCESS RAVONNA, WHO TEETERS ON THE VERGE OF BEING WIPED FROM EXISTENCE.

KANG WILL STOP AT NOTHING TO RESTORE HIS TIME LINE AND RAVONNA, EVEN IF IT MEANS DESTROYING THE AVENGERS AND CONQUERING THE ENTIRE WORLD.

# BARON STRUCKER

## NAME: WOLFGANG VON STRUCKER

BORN IN THE EARLY 1900S TO A NOBLE PRUSSIAN FAMILY WHO HAD RELOCATED TO STRUCKER CASTLE IN BAVARIA FOLLOWING THE FRANCO-PRUSSIAN WAR, WOLFGANG VON STRUCKER BECAME A HEIDELBERG FENCING CHAMPION. IN WORLD WAR II HE SERVED AS LIEUTENANT TO HYDRA'S SUPER-SOLDIER, THE RED SKULL.

OVER THE YEARS, STRUCKER HAS CLIMBED FAR UP THE RANKS OF HYDRA, EVEN TAKING CONTROL OF THE ORGANIZATION AND CLAIMING THE TITLE OF BARON WHEN ZEMO WAS IMPRISONED BY S.H.I.E.L.D.

DURING ONE OF HYDRA'S MISSIONS TO ACQUIRE LOST RELICS OF THE OCCULT, STRUCKER CAME INTO POSSESSION OF A GAUNTLET OF IMMENSE POWER. ALTHOUGH IT COST STRUCKER HIS RIGHT ARM, THE GAUNTLET HAS GIVEN HIM THE ABILITY TO SAP ANOTHER PERSON'S LIFE FORCE, ABSORBING IT INTO HIMSELF AND THEREBY KEEPING HIMSELF YOUNG AND STRONG.

# LOKI

BORN THE SON OF THE KING OF THE FROST GIANTS, LOKI WAS ADOPTED BY ODIN AND RAISED AS A BROTHER TO ODIN'S BIOLOGICAL SON, THOR. LOKI GREW UP RESENTING HIS BROTHER AND THE FACT THAT ALL OF MYTHICAL ASGARD SEEMED TO FAVOR THOR. HE TURNED TO SORCERY AND THE ARTS OF TRICKERY, BOTH OF WHICH HE HAD A NATURAL AFFINITY FOR. AS HE MATURED, THE MISCHIEF HE CAUSED GREW TO BECOME EVIL.

NOW LOKI WILL STOP AT NOTHING TO CAUSE TROUBLE FOR HIS ADOPTED BROTHER.

# CHARACTER PROFILES

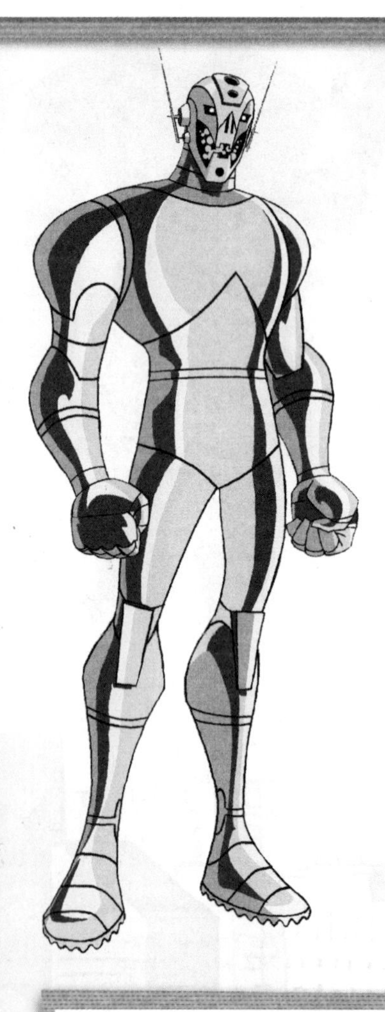

## ULTRON

Long ago, Hank Pym and Tony Stark worked together to create a new robotic AI with human brain waves mapped onto a computer. When Hank found out that Tony intended to sell it as a weapon, he scrapped the project...but desperate times forced Hank to bring Ultron back online. Programmed to protect humanity, Ultron's AI is so advanced that its only logical solution to saving the human race...is to control it. No matter the cost.

## ENCHANTRESS

Amora, the Enchantress, is one of the most powerful sorceresses in all the Nine Realms. Although she hails from the realm known as Vanaheim, she honed her magical abilities in Asgard, and — while residing there — developed an affection for the mighty Thor. After a series of unrequited attempts to capture his heart, however, Amora began to nurture a deep spite for the Thunderer, as well as for any female unwise enough to capture his eye. This has driven the Enchantress to throw her lot in with Loki, Thor's manipulative step-brother, who also seeks vengeance on the mighty one.

## CRIMSON DYNAMO

### NAME: IVAN VANKO

A Soviet scientist of Armenian birth with a PhD in physics, Vanko was one of the world's unsung geniuses. He built a powered exoskeleton capable of performing incredible feats on par with that of his self-proclaimed nemesis, Tony Stark. Seeking to settle the grudge that his father held against his one-time collaborator and Tony's father, Howard Stark, Ivan is determined to bring down Iron Man once and for all.

## ABOMINATION

### NAME: EMIL BLONSKY

Formerly known as Emil Blonsky, a special forces operative trained by the British SAS, the Abomination gained his powers after receiving a dose of gamma radiation similar to that which transformed Bruce Banner into the Incredible Hulk. As a result he was permanently transformed into a massive green-skinned monster whose physical power was equivalent to, if not greater than, that of the Hulk. While he was able to maintain his normal level of self-control and intelligence after this transformation, he is unable to return to human form. Given his gamma-spawned origins, Blonsky blames his condition on Banner and his alter ego, the Hulk.

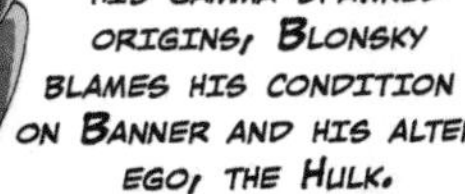

# CHARACTER PROFILES

# HAWKEYE'S BAG OF TRICKS

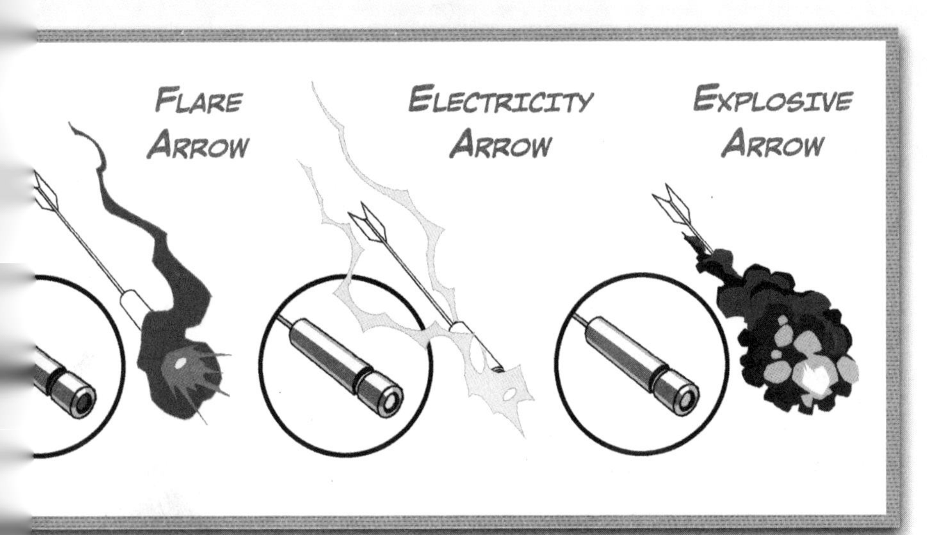

## ARROWS

# AVENGERS' FILES

## THE MIGHTY MJOLNIR!

THOR'S HAMMER WAS COMMISSIONED BY HIS FATHER ODIN AND FORGED BY DWARVES. WITH IT, HE CAN FLY AS WELL AS BEND LIGHTING TO HIS WILL – CALLING DOWN MASSIVE LIGHTNING STRIKES WITH GREAT PRECISION AND POWER.

THE HAMMER ALWAYS RETURNS TO HIM ONCE THROWN. ITS MAGIC GIVES THE THUNDERER ACCESS TO THE RAINBOW BRIDGE, THE PORTAL TO ASGARD, AND, MOST NOTABLY, CANNOT BE PICKED UP BY ANY WHO ARE NOT DEEMED WORTHY, NO MATTER THEIR STRENGTH.

# IN EVIL HANDS!

HEY, TRUE BELIEVER! CAN YOU NAME THE NEFARIOUS OWNERS OF THESE WRATHFUL WEAPONS? (ANSWERS BELOW, FOR YA FACT CHECKERS!)

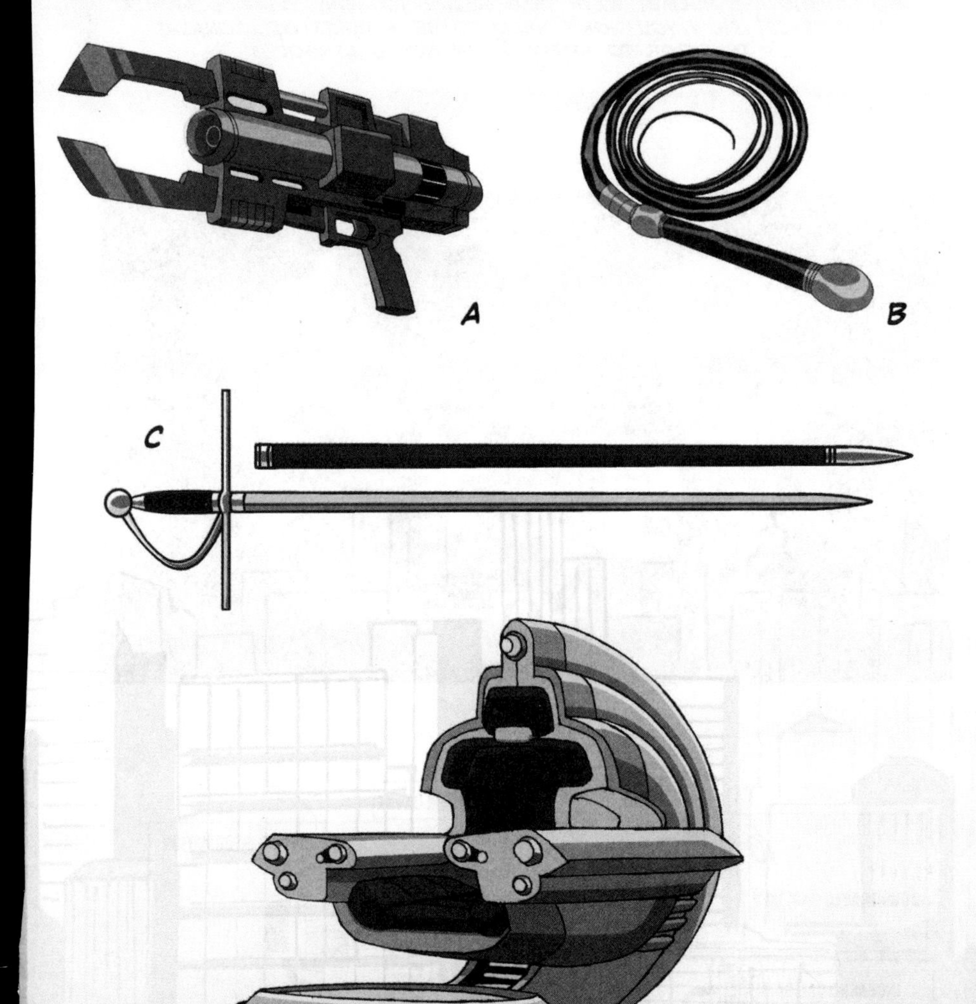


A) A.I.M. ANTI-GRAVITY GUN
B) WHIPLASH'S WHIP
C) BARON ZEMO'S ANCESTRAL SWORD
D) KANG'S TIME-CHAIR

# AVENGERS' FILES

## BREAKING DOWN THE HUD!

GO BEHIND THE HELMET WITH THIS GUIDE TO TONY STARK'S ARMOR INTERFACE! NOW YOU DON'T NEED TO BE A MULTI-BILLIONAIRE INVENTOR TO SPEAK IRON MAN'S LINGO!

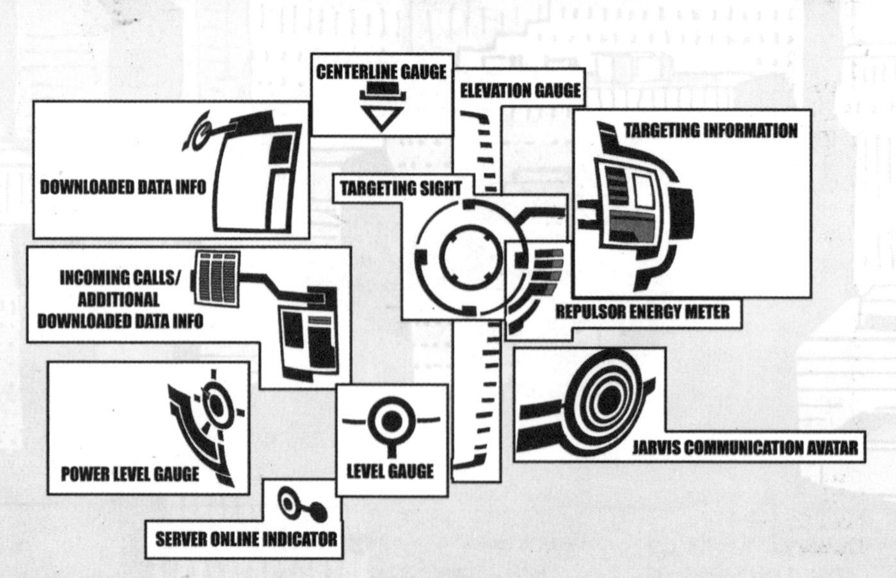